Beneath Me

Super Love, Volume 1.5

SE White

Published by SE White, 2021.

BENEATH ME

First edition. September 30, 2021.

Copyright © 2021 SE White.

ISBN: 979-8201891381

Written by SE White.

To the monster lovers group on #Romancestagram. I hope
Marcelline is your kind of monster. And for the romance
readers who love it when a villain gets the happy ending. I love
it, too.

Table of Contents

Chapter One...1

Chapter Two..5

Chapter Three 9

Chapter Four 15

Chapter Five 19

Chapter Six 23

Chapter Seven 29

Chapter Eight 35

Chapter Nine...41

Chapter Ten 45

Sneak Preview: The Sidekick and The Supervillain, by SE White . 49

Chapter One

Water Wonder snuck up the beach in a wobbly crouch so unlike his customary confident strut that any of his paparazzi would have doubted he *could* be the oceanic superhero.

Image was everything, and it drove him hard but here—far offshore—he had no image. Inside his hidden cavern he could enjoy the unsteady way wet sand sucked at each footstep. If he tripped, he could go ahead and fall. Frigid hells, he could get sand up his nose, and *not one person would see.*

He could let the constant maintenance of Water Wonder's identity dissolve for a while and become plain Caspian Barbeau. No worries. No filling out his super suit with perfect muscles, flawless hair, and ideal heroic attitude at all times. No desperately battling to keep the forces of Evil at bay. No responsibilities.

A gurgly, questioning chirp came from the pile of crumbled basalt to his right, and he immediately headed that way. No responsibilities down here—except one.

On the walls phosphorescent algae lit the murky cave with a greenish-teal glow. He'd planted just enough for his ocean-adapted eyes. Any more would have annoyed and blinded him like the surface sunlight did. Through the entrance tunnel he could hear the ocean, but muted, the power of the sound tamped down by the rocks surrounding him.

He approached the basalt and cooed, "Hi, buddy. Hey. Are you hiding? Wanna come out?"

Scratching came from behind the rocks, then stopped. Nothing moved but the water giving quick, salty smacks to the tiny beach.

He sat on the patio cushion stashed in front of the tumble of rocks and leaned his back against one of the larger, more algae covered ones. This far inside his cave the sand was slightly damp instead of dripping wet. It made the cushion even softer. Tipping his head back, Caspian sighed happily and closed his eyes, relaxing into the quiet dark and the feeling of being blissfully alone.

After a while, he broke the tranquil silence. "I nicked a few smelts on the way in. You could have them. If you want to come out here."

More scraping. Then another chirp, this one enthusiastic. Caspian didn't open his eyes until he felt the hard prickle of legs on his shoulder and Rex dropped into his lap. Which meant forty five pounds of greenish-brown, hard-carapaced lobster landed on his groin.

"*Fuck*," he huffed, then glanced around the dark, quiet cave guiltily. "You weigh a ton. I don't think you need these smelt. I think you need a diet."

Rex ignored his comment utterly, poking a commanding pincher claw at Caspian's right-side pocket. The tip dug into his skintight super suit.

Caspian pulled out the two slimy fish he'd zipped safely inside and held them up above the lobster's tallest antennae. "What do you say? What do you say to get snacks?" He wiggled the fish enticingly.

Rex squeaked, then made a string of *clicking* noises which sounded like a broken clockwork landing cog-by-cog on a tile floor. Salty bubbles grew and popped around his food handling appendages and the tiny black dots of his eyes wiggled on their short stalks. For the finale, he snapped the tips of his wide crusher claw together and gestured towards himself.

It was the cutest thing Caspian had seen for days and he chuckled as he handed over the treats. "*Such* a good boy. Good job. You're communicating! Yes, you are."

A sultry voice sliced through the moment. "You spoil your pets rotten."

Caspian jolted so hard his hand knocked into Rex, who swatted him warningly with his crusher claw. He'd know that melodic voice anywhere, above or below the waves. "Sea Bitch? H-how did . . . I mean, what are you doing? Here?"

He popped to his feet and stepped in front of his pet. As if he could somehow hide a lobster the size of a small dog whose antennae reached as high as his knees. Rex tried to scuttle out from behind him and he sidestepped to block. "Did we have a battle scheduled for today?"

"What do you think?"

He imagined Sea Bitch gave him a scathing look. They were a specialty of hers. But he kept his attention on Rex so he could pretend he wasn't desperately aware his nemesis stood so close. In *his* space.

The lobster tried the other direction, but Caspian blocked him again. "Yeah, well, I don't have one in my phone. No alarm set, um, d-did I forget?" Rex smacked into the back of his calf, making him stagger forward one awkward step. Then the little stinker darted around him, moving at top lobster speed.

Caspian sighed in defeat. *Hope he pinches her really hard.*

Until this moment the isolated cave—with a long underwater tunnel no regular breathing person could access—had been his refuge from everything. *Including* his nemesis.

"Look, I'm not ready for a battle today. I've got nothing. Can we pick this up tomorrow? I . . . " he trailed off, watching *his* pet lobster rub enthusiastically against one of Sea Bitch's larger tentacles. The cheeky little brat popped more bubbles and waved both claws expressively while the greatest Evil Being in the ocean gave him an adoring smile.

Caspian had never seen such a soft look on her face before.

Chapter Two

The Sea Bitch was no normal woman. Instead of human legs, she rose on nine bunched tentacles that reminded Caspian strongly of an octopus. Firm with muscle, each one started out as thick as his thigh. Their dark purple color contrasted starkly with her lavender colored skin and shades-of-blue hair. He intimately knew the power of those tentacles because he'd been smacked by every single one. Numerous times. She could send him, a full grown man, ankles-over-arse into the closest wall with minimal effort.

If she decided to slap Rex with even the single wrist-sized tip he was now affectionately patting, she could turn him into a jellied smear. Caspian leaned forward with his hands extended, wondering if he'd be able to snatch Rex before that happened. Although they were big, her tentacles moved with predatory speed.

"Stop tensing at me like that," she said calmly. "I don't go around squashing harmless lobsters for no reason." She darted her gaze to meet his and put on a mocking smile, showing the sharp tips of her teeth. "Not even the ones *Wonder What's Water Boy* keeps as a pet."

He rolled his eyes. "Water Wonder. *Wah-ter, wohn-der.* You really should know the name of the superhero who kicked your ass last week."

A brief flicker of emotion crossed her face, causing a needle sharp sting between his ribs although he didn't know . . . why. Before he could register the startling pain her usual icy expression had returned. "And *you* really should know better than to provoke the villain who kicked *your* watery ass the week before that."

Caspian tried to force away the dull heat he could feel spreading across his cheeks. She *had* beaten him badly two weeks ago. She'd slammed him so hard into the railings underneath Ocean City Pier he'd seen starbursts, and his gills hadn't been able to pull in enough oxygen for a moment. He was fairly sure he *still* had barnacle imprints on his back.

Sea Bitch looked away, dismissing Caspian from her personal universe. The tentacle Rex had been investigating curled around him and lifted the lobster effortlessly into her arms. Although her legs were pure sea-creature Sea Bitch was human from the waist up. She cuddled Caspian's pet, dropping a kiss on that hard, spiny carapace and Rex The Traitor, Last of His Name burbled happily.

The power of the open ocean called to Caspian and every one of his muscles tensed. All that water waited only a tunnel's length behind her. One twitch of his hand and he could call it. Bring a wave to pin her down until she surrendered and stopped fighting, as he had last week. Or he could create a sucking current to drag her out of his cave. His *sanctuary*, dammit.

He really, *really* wished that after three years of fighting his archrival he had learned to ignore Sea Bitch's breasts. Alas, they were flawless. Perfectly proportioned to her statuesque torso, beautifully fitted in the tight, navy blue top she always wore to cover her human half. Rex was snuggled right up against them. Lucky little booger.

"Just—would you give me back my lobster," he demanded. She bent over and placed Rex on the ground without argument, and his head jerked back in surprise. Guiltily, he dragged his gaze away from the neckline of her top and snapped his fingers. "Come here, Rex. C'mere, little guy."

"Girl."

"What?"

"Rex. She's female. Did you never check?"

Caspian stared at Sea Bitch while his favorite lobster scooted across the sand to him. "No," he mumbled. "I never did." Rex butted his—her head against his leg and he reached down to pat her carefully on her spiny shell.

"She doesn't care, really. Gender isn't a big deal to lobsters." The Sea Bitch kept any judgmental inflections suggesting he could be a much more attentive pet owner out of her voice, which he appreciated. "And she's happy to have the name Rex. She thinks it sounds sharp and scary."

Rex squeaked.

"Threatening," she amended.

Satisfied, Rex wandered back towards her rock lair, investigating the sand for any specks of food as she went.

"You can talk with Rex?" Caspian asked. How had he never known this about his adversary?

"Sea creatures," Sea Bitch explained. She sounded weary, the complete opposite of the emotion Caspian would be feeling if *he* could understand the animals who inhabited his beloved ocean. "I'm a creature of the sea so I understand sea beasts. I am not Hero Doolittle, or some shit. I don't do land animals. Don't ask."

"I wasn't going to. I have no interest in land animals." Sad, but true. The friends who owned and adored fluffy dogs or twittery birds only baffled Caspian.

A smile bloomed on the villain's face, as unexpectedly bright as a bioluminescent wave. "That's something we have in common," she said. Humor turned her already musical voice into a rich, seductive melody.

Caspian stared, a little dazed.

She . . . somehow amidst all the banter and being battered underneath her tentacles, he had gotten into the habit of overlooking the facts. And the facts were, Sea Bitch was indisputably gorgeous. That razor sharp, beautifully sculpted bone structure easily eclipsed an ocean sunset. And the thought was true without *also* considering her curves, her pouty purple lips, or her amazing, thickly-lashed violet eyes.

"You have a name, don't you?" he asked, before his brain could rev back to working speed. "You're not just . . . the Sea Bitch all the time." A superhero would *never* outright ask for his nemesis to reveal their secret identity. Lesson one, day one at Riverdale Powers Preparatory. Where he'd honestly hated every moment stuck in a classroom, away from the ocean.

If he hadn't been stunned witless by her smile, he would have kept to the rules. Like he always had.

"I have a name," she confirmed, one slender eyebrow cocked disdainfully. That genuine, pretty smile disappeared. "Will I give it to you? No. I don't expect you to hand over yours."

"Caspian," he blurted. "My name is Caspian."

She closed her eyes and inhaled, slowly. "Why?" she demanded. Her tentacles writhed over and around themselves like a pit of anxious anacondas. "Why do you have to make this harder than it already is? Damn you."

Chapter Three

Marcelline kept her eyes closed so she wouldn't have to look at *Caspian*, because she'd already tortured herself enough for one day. And now he'd gone and added to the anguish. An upper limit to what she could endure *had* to exist. Somewhere. But she couldn't seem to find it.

Caspian. His name was Caspian. Such a *perfect* name.

Damn the man straight to the darkest deep.

The first time she'd seen him, underneath the boat she'd been in the process of sabotaging, both of her hearts had skipped two different beats. Even her tentacles had stilled, as if they knew the moment was special. The thought had come out of nowhere—*mine. This one is for me.*

He'd swum towards her without a scuba suit or breathing tubes, nearly ten meters underwater and *kilometers* away from shore. With no more protection than a skintight aquamarine super suit, he'd cut through Marcelline's element with confident grace.

Clearly he belonged under the waves. Just like her. She'd never met anyone else who did. Only him, this beautiful man with black hair and sea blue eyes swimming to her. After literally being spawned in a tank as the product of a deranged evil scientist trying to create an army of sea creatures, raised like an experiment, and finally watching Ballina eat their "father" when his trials went too far . . . wasn't Marcelline owed one small kindness from the universe? Only one?

Apparently not, because he'd opened that posh mouth, cocked an eyebrow, and said, *"What's a villain like you doing in a deep zone like this?"*

A sudden, vicious current had ripped into her out of nowhere, tossing her away. Stunned, she'd instinctively kept hold of the anchor chain she'd been in the process of breaking. Not only the chain, but the entire roller and windlass—plus a hefty portion of deck—had come with her, and the boat had started to sink. Which, alright, yes, she'd intended to do anyway but she'd *meant* to start a slow leak which would force the damn thing to limp back to shore. Not to capsize it.

She'd lashed out in defense, herding him away with careful strikes from her tentacles. Somehow he'd managed to dodge every single one. Eventually, she'd started to understand it was *him* controlling the water around her, *him* shoving her this way and that like a piece of litter in a strong current.

"What's going on? What is wrong *with you?"* she'd demanded.

He'd only growled, *"Enough! Shove off! I have to save those fishermen. I* don't want them to drown," obviously implying that she did.

In that moment, she'd understood. He come with her already pre-judged as a person-killer. An enemy. The villain. Instantly she'd spun away and left him to rescue his precious shark-murderers, pushing her tentacles harder than she ever had in her life.

But she wasn't able to stay away from him. Her nemesis, her ocean rival, her *obsession*. From that day their roles had been defined. He was Water Wonder, the golden hero who walked in the dry sunshine, which irritated her tentacles unbearably. He was so popular the land creatures had made a *movie* about him. Whereas she was Sea Bitch, the monster who made two-leggers scream at the sight of her. The evil thing from the scary deep ocean who fought him.

Also being utterly obsessed with the hero was her own pathetic secret.

"Um. Sea Bitch?" he said tentatively, snapping her back to the present. "Is something wrong?"

No. Ohh, no. He did not get to sound all soft and maybe even a touch worried about her. After three long years of battles he did not get to treat her like she had *feelings* or reveal his name as if it meant nothing.

Like always when she was near Water Wonder her ribs felt as if they would crackle inward, compressing her chest until she thought her hearts might surrender.

As she'd learned to do over three long years of practice, she transformed the ruin of her insides into pure action.

She snapped her eyes open and lunged, knocking Water Wonder over. He hit the sand and rolled, cursing.

The familiarity of the fight grounded her, settling her sore stomach. *This* was her life since Water Wonder had come into it. Reflex shot three of her tentacles out to stop him. Her tentacles saw *prey* and *escaping* and acted without her guidance. Instantly Water Wonder reversed course, scrambling, sand flying around his hands. Another tentacle intercepted and smacked so roughly he tumbled onto his back. She didn't often catch the superhero off-guard like this and truthfully had no idea what to do, beyond *make him hurt like I hurt right now.*

He started to scoot backward, evading the flailing limbs which had taken on a life of their own. With no conscious direction from her, the two tentacles nearest to him wrapped around his wrists like manacles. They slammed his arms to the ground. His head bounced, and wet sand clung to his dark hair as he glared daggers at her.

She slapped her hands against his chest to push, going along with her tentacle's impulse. They seemed to have the right idea here. He writhed and kicked out with his legs so she deliberately sent another two tentacles to smother them.

"Quit it!" he barked.

"Why?" She could barely breathe, so talking was an effort. *Crack, crack,* crack. There went the rest of her ribs, her chest, her windpipe. Pushed against the hot weight of him, her palms jumped with each heaving breath he took. His irreplaceable single heart thrummed against her palms.

"I don't want to fight you right now." He twisted and strained, trying to budge her grip. He might as well have been pinned under the boulders Rex currently crouched on, watching them with beady-eyed interest.

"You do." *You always do.*

Shockingly cold water splashed against her back, but nowhere near the power or amount he usually used to battle. Why wasn't he wrapping a wave around her to force her off of him?

"Fight me!" she hissed.

"No."

She leaned down until her face was only an inch from his. Until the air escaping his lungs brushed against her lips, and she inhaled the salty, sweet scent of him. Their bodies touched from shoulders to the tips of her tentacles and his toes. Ache, she ached all over and she wanted but couldn't have. She couldn't even *pretend* she'd ever get more than this.

"Fight. Back."

"No." Bright, hot excitement dropped over his features. But his seawater eyes were . . . softer than she'd ever seen them.

How dare he. How fucking *dare* he.

Marcelline tensed, preparing to heave herself off of him and leave. She couldn't. Her tentacles—stubborn things—locked in place and wouldn't allow her to move. They had a mind of their own, a network of neurons unconnected to her human brain. But a few sensory cells didn't make them intelligent enough to understand why she could not have this man. Their desire to absorb the scent-taste of his skin and never let him go was merely a stupid impulse.

His head moved closer, slow, slow, while his soft gaze focused on her mouth.

She stopped breathing entirely. *Oh, please. Please. Please.*

Their lips touched.

She knew only vaguely what this involved from catching glimpses of couples having a romantic evening on the beach. Superpowered humans weren't exactly lining up to lock lips with a gilled, purple villain and as for regular unpowered people? She was lucky if they didn't back away, laughing nervously when they saw her.

In her wildest, most covert fantasies she'd imagined Water Wonder somehow longing to kiss her and known she'd be embarrassed by her lack of experience. In actuality, the soft pressure and the overwhelming feeling of his body against hers dashed any notion of humiliation away. She had no time to worry when her entire being was swept up in kissing her nemesis. All she could do was vaguely remember to suck in some air and get her lungs working again.

They moved together like they couldn't stop fighting. Even in this moment. She couldn't take control of the kiss because he kept stealing it back by nipping, teasing, *licking*. She hadn't known about the licking. Or that the short, bristly hairs on his face would prick her skin, even when they were hard to see.

Her hands wouldn't keep still. They wandered, tracing the shape of his chest muscles, his shoulders, the curve of his neck, his face. Everything she'd memorized from afar. She was *touching his face* and he was *letting* her and nothing in her world made sense anymore. She'd been knocked reeling by shorebreak she hadn't seen coming.

Sucking in more desperately needed oxygen, she moaned. "Again. Do that again. More."

"Oh . . . no," he said, the words rough and broken against her lips. "Oh, fuck me, your sexy *voice*. What are we going to do now?" He sucked on her lower lip and then bit down, panting.

His shaking hands came to rest on either side of her neck and she wondered when her tentacles had let him go. It didn't matter. As long as he kept touching her. Her pulse raced at quadruple time beneath his fingers. Excitement flowered inside her, brand new and utterly overpowering.

Her breasts had never felt so full, so sensitive. As if he knew, Caspian's hands trailed down her throat. He rubbed his palms against the stiff points of her nipples, back and forth through her top. She arched to bring them closer to him. "*Yes*. Just like that. Yes."

"What are we doing right now?" he groaned, his fingers tightening around her breasts. "Sea Bitch?"

His voice held only stunned question. No condemnation, no malice at all. That was the only name he knew her by.

She couldn't *stand* to hear it.

Her tentacles recoiled, and she scrambled off of him.

Caspian sat up. His hair stuck out in the random tufts left by her hands, and his lips were puffy and swollen from her kisses. The mating part of him she'd never seen jutted, clearly outlined by his tight suit. She hadn't dared to acknowledge how hot and heavy it had felt pressed against her abdomen just seconds before.

"We're supposed to battle," she snarled. To her own ears her voice sounded as if she'd been scraping her throat with salt. "That is not fighting. Do it again and I'll pin you to a reef for the crabs."

"What? *You* knocked *me* over and held me down." Now he sounded angry. Finally.

"And you *kissed* me," she retorted.

"I—well, yeah. I did." He blinked. "Maybe I want us to try again. Without getting pinned to a reef. We don't . . . have to fight all the time." He looked like he couldn't believe the words coming from his own mouth.

Maybe I'd fight the entire damn ocean to do that some more. But it. Will never. Happen. "I am the Sea Bitch." She tore the words from her throat to fling them at him. Her eyes stung so she lifted her chin. He would not see her cry. "That's all I ever have been to you. That's all I ever will be. Do *not* forget it."

Before she could do anything humiliating, like begging him to forget what she'd just said and kiss her all over again, Marcelline turned her back to him and dove into the water.

Chapter Four

The sun had barely started to peek over the horizon the next morning as Caspian swam a few kilometers out from the shoreline south of Ocean City. He ducked in and out of the water compulsively, searching each crest above, every sand plain beneath him. Small wavelets splashed in his face, making him blink.

He'd told himself all morning he was patrolling. Only patrolling. Rushing through his shower, wolfing down a protein bar, pretending he was in a hurry to start his route watching over the stretch of ocean he considered his. Searching for the Sea Bitch because that was part of his daily responsibilities.

He'd tried over and over to tell himself that, but sadly himself turned out to be a huge liar.

Something urgent drummed through his chest, driving him to hurry, *hurry*, locking down until he could barely gulp in water for his gills. She could disappear so easily, and he'd never find her if she didn't want to be found. Sea Bitch was a hundred times more at home in the ocean than him.

That's all I ever have been to you.

Well, damn it, if he knew what else to call her, he would use that name.

That's all I ever will be.

Hearing those defeated words in her smooth, lyrical voice had hit him like a shard of coral to the guts. Especially when that voice had been huskier than he'd ever heard it before, roughened by his mouth on hers, his touches. Everything about their interaction yesterday had been brand new and, if he were honest, he wanted to keep exploring it. Now he knew a truth—they didn't have to fight all of the time.

Yesterday had reframed *everything* for him. What if it hadn't for her?

He ducked underwater to scan the sea floor again, letting his eyes adjust to the comparative dimness. As he did, he flexed his chest and inhaled slowly, feeling water spread through the gills tucked on each side of his abdomen, the same way cold dribbles of rain would slide across a windowpane. A chilly, soft current flowed around him as he swam.

The largest kelp forest on this coastline lay ahead. There would almost certainly be divers in it. Maritimas Oceanographic Institute, located on the shore by the famous Ocean City lighthouse, sent regular teams to study the surrounding ecosystems. Maybe they'd seen her. People were usually too happy to inform him of the Sea Bitch's movements, as if being a telltale was heroic.

That's all I ever have been to you.

He jerked his head to the side, trying to drive off the words.

Three years ago the Smallcity Legion of Heroes had dispatched him as a solo hero, with the instructions to 'stop the villain sinking boats outside Ocean City'. Brand-squeaky-new, nineteen years old, five days out from graduation at Riverdale Prep, and still unused to answering to his own superhero name.

Over the years Caspian had settled into being Water Wonder, Defender of the Sea, Ocean City's Most Eligible Bachelor, and movie star. People's perceptions molded him into their champion and he'd even been *grateful* for it, at first. If people said he was a hero, then he acted like one. He must be one. And what was any hero without their nemesis? Just someone with superpowers poncing around in a tight suit.

He'd patrolled every day for years driven by the prickly urge to find his adversary. To see her, speak with her, banter a bit. Sometimes fight, but never seriously enough to injure her. Never that. They'd had their daily routine, and he'd never named the simple emotion driving him to come back every time. *Concern.* He worried about her.

His fingers clenched, craving her smooth, slippery skin underneath them again. His wrists tingled, missing the binding hold of her tentacles. Before yesterday, he hadn't known how *good* that would feel.

Sleep had laughed and waved a middle finger at him most of the night while he wondered where she could be hiding and exactly how angry she was with him for kissing her. If she still looked as sad as she had when she left his cave. If she was safe.

Inside the underwater forest, the only clear directions were *up* and *down*. Towards the light or towards the holdfasts clinging in the gloom beneath. Everything else became a matter of perspective, distances transformed into fractured fragments of sunlight and shade.

He easily picked out the rising bubble trails which meant divers using scuba gear and shifted direction to intercept them. But a shadowy outline cutting through the kelp made him stop dead in the water. *Shark. Dirty great* big *one*.

Many species of sharks lived off this rich coastline. Usually, Caspian had no problem with them. He gave them the respect they'd earned as an apex predator and left them alone unless they were a clear threat to human life. They were extremely intelligent. After Caspian had shoved them away from swimmers with his strong currents a few times they'd seemed to learn that people were off-limits for snackies.

No shark should be this close to the divers. No shark should be swimming through a kelp forest, divers or not. They had no room to maneuver inside the close-growing, tangly fronds. It wasn't normal behavior. And no shark he'd ever seen before was this *massive*. It had to be six, maybe even seven, meters long.

Caspian gulped so hard seawater stung his throat.

Quietly he swam towards the giant thing, gathering his power. Reassuring force built around his body, surging him forward, growing like a bubble. When he popped it he could send the shark flying back out to the deep sea.

A hauntingly familiar voice murmured softly from his left. "No. I said no. Those stretchy suits would make you sick. You know . . ." she trailed off without finishing the thought aloud.

Caspian rounded a feathery kelp frond and saw her. Sea Bitch had a hand stretched out in front of the shark's nose, floating perhaps a meter away from it. Her expression was serene, as if she spoke firmly to giant predators all the time. Maybe she did, he had no way of knowing.

"You barely fit in here, anyway. Why don't you go back out where it's deep?" she asked.

The shark shifted one doorknob-sized eye to stare at the Sea Bitch. A terrifyingly pointy mouth gaped in the *furthest* thing from a smile, teeth glittering in the refracted underwater sunlight. Caspian couldn't hear a sound, but Sea Bitch was clearly listening carefully to something.

"Ballina. I'm fine."

The creature's massive tail fin swished from side-to-side. It seemed to be part of the shark's answer, but Caspian got caught in the unexpected surge it created. He slipped further out of the kelp frond's shadow, waving his arms to try and stay in place.

Sea Bitch caught sight of him. She froze. Those matchless purple eyes widened.

In a split second the shark whirled and came for him. No posturing, no pretend charge. Massive shark wanted to eat and it *would* eat him if he didn't move.

Caspian threw out his arms with an uncontrolled, panicked blast of water. He managed to nudge the giant animal aside. Barely. A pectoral fin clipped him as the shark swept by, drawing a bloodied line across his check.

Chapter Five

"Ballina, no! Don't!" Marcelline cried out, too panicked to remember she didn't need to use her voice. Her friend would hear her thoughts like always, but fear foamed over her like a wave.

She pushed against the wake left by Caspian's power, raking her arms through the water, trying to reach him.

::*This one. This hurtful, oblivious one. I'll make him sorry::* the thought blasted into Marcelline's head.

She winced. ::*NO don't hurt him::* she tried again, hurling the thought as desperately as she threw herself through the water. Her lungs ached. The ocean seemed to be backing up in her gills as her hearts hammered. She wasn't close enough. "No," she croaked.

Ballina ignored her and rushed Caspian, her mouth gaping wide, and her pupils rolled back in attack mode. Again, he barely evaded, shoving the massive creature with a swell of seawater and rolling himself sideways. The cut on his cheek trickled a tiny red trail after him.

Sharply, Ballina sent ::*He is too stupid to make you a proper mate anyway. He doesn't protect you, cherish you, treat you as he should::* Clear resentment flavored her mind-tone. Marcelline wasted a split second she didn't have to *wish* she hadn't confided her unrequited feelings to Ballina so many times.

::*He will never do any of those things if you EAT him. Please, please don't!::*

Caspian tried to duck behind one of the larger fronds of kelp, clutching and pulling so hard the entire column swayed. Ballina's mouth split in a malicious smile. She angled her body, then dove far enough that Marcelline could hardly make her out near the seafloor.

Marcelline drove herself harder, harder, aiming for Caspian's kicking legs. She reached him barely in time, as Ballina came hurtling towards the superhero, like an unstoppable tsunami. The kelp around her massive body shifted and tossed as if a wild storm had somehow gotten underwater.

Marcelline spun to face the shark with her arms out wide, all of her tentacles flared in a threatening halo. Caspian grasped her waist, and she thought he might be trying to move her aside but there wasn't enough time. If he said anything she couldn't hear it through the blood roaring in her ears.

At the very last moment, Ballina turned aside. A sharp flare of agony burst in Marcelline's leftmost tentacle as the slipstream caused by the shark's passage sent both Marcelline and Caspian spinning. She grabbed frantically for any kelp nearby, ripping the first two out before she slowed enough to grab a third.

Then Ballina was gone, slipping into the gloom in the direction of the edge of the underwater forest. Her parting words floated over Marcelline ::*I would not eat such a pale sickly thing*:: she sent. ::*Even if he deserves it. I only wanted to scare him a little*::

::*I'm positive you scared him a lot*:: Marcelline sent back, wryly.

Caspian's hands landed on her shoulders. He tugged her around to face him. "What in all the frigid hells was that?" This far underwater his voice was muffled, as though her ears were stuffed. It was harder to speak here, but not impossible, and both of them had the ability.

His sea blue eyes raked from her head to the tips of her tentacle limbs. The cut on his cheek had already stopped bleeding. "What happened? Are you alrigh—oh hells, no, you're not. You're *hurt*."

Surprised, she looked down. A little cloud of navy blue ichor bloomed around the end of one of her tentacles. Or rather, what *had* been the end of her tentacle. "Oh," she said vaguely.

A chunk nearly the length of her forearm had disappeared, sliced off by Ballina's massive teeth as she swept by. Surely an accident in the heat of the moment. In the saltwater it stung as if someone had shoved it in a fire and held it there.

"Your poor tentacle," Caspian said, sounding anguished. He lifted the mangled limb, cupping it in one palm, then stroked tenderly up to the edge of the damage with his other hand. "Oh, poor thing. Does it hurt?"

Hurt? What? Marcelline stilled, trapped motionless by a potent mixture of yearning and awe and shock. No one had ever touched her tentacles before. No one. Not voluntarily. People could hardly stand *looking* at her, but somehow, Caspian willingly put his hands on her. His fingers brushed against her suckers as if they didn't disgust him.

She stared at his dark hair as he bent his head over her in concern, while her blood turned the water around them hazy. Her suckers relayed the delicious scent-taste of his skin to her, curling a little with happiness. Then, he tilted his head. His eyes meeting hers felt like an actual blow to the chest.

"Does it hurt?" he asked again.

"No," she said in complete honesty. With his touch, his fingers against her skin, nothing hurt at all, except her heart.

Chapter Six

Muffled movement and the *whoosh-hiss* of escaping bubbles penetrated Marcelline's awareness. Instinctively, she spun to face the threat. Caspian's hands slipped away from her torn limb and she mourned the loss. Especially when only the ocean institute divers in their scuba suits swam into view. They circled the holdfast of one of the kelp strands, poking at it with little glass tubes, blissfully unaware of the struggle and the giant predator which had come within meters of them.

They loved the ocean, respected its creatures, and generally, Marcelline liked them as much as she could any two-legger. But right now she wished them all to trench depths. They would see her if they bothered to look around, which meant her time with Water Wonder was over for today. All of her tentacles thrashed and contracted, once, disgusted with the thought.

He wrapped an arm around her waist from behind. With a soft push of water, he maneuvered her away, further into the kelp fronds until the divers disappeared from view. The ocean swirled around them in familiar rhythm, cradling them together.

"What are you–" she began.

"We're not finished here," he said quietly. "We need to talk about you throwing yourself in front of a shark for me. And getting hurt doing it."

"We don't need to discuss a thing," she retorted, forcing bravado into her tone. Most of her brain function was fixated on reveling in the sensation of his hands on her sides. "I'm fine. It'll grow back." *In six months. Maybe a year.*

She'd do it again, without a thought. Fight him, follow him, protect him. Anything. Her tentacles curled in on themselves in disgrace. She was so pitiful for this man, and he didn't even realize it.

"It's fine." She tried to turn, push away, get some space between them so he wouldn't notice her battered hearts being tugged around on a string behind him.

But he banded his strong arms around her stomach, holding her in place. His chest pressed against her back like an unyielding wall. Her tentacles wrapped around his legs, ready to peel him off of her, but she directed them to wait.

"It's not fine," he growled. "Not. Fine. None of this is fine. You got hurt defending me." The sensation of his lips against the sensitive curve of her ear made her shiver. He rubbed gentle circles on her stomach in a soothing motion, dropping his hand lower with every pass. Lower. *Lower.*

Sweet, thick tension throbbed through her veins, and she wanted to explore it a little more before she yanked him away. She couldn't help but to push into the cradle of his thighs. Somehow, yes, there was his erection thickening behind her. He gave her a slight pump of his hips in return.

Ruthlessly, she smothered the whimper trying to crawl out of her.

"I'm not—I don't know what to do. This is brand new for us," he said. "But I know I don't want to battle with you anymore. I definitely don't want to see you bleed, ever again." Convulsively, his arms tightened around her.

Did he . . . care what happened to her? Had she somehow missed the signs all these years?

At her back his chest moved quickly, propelled by his breath. "I should probably be asking you about the giant shark that just tried to kill me."

She scrunched up her nose. *About that. Um.*

"But all I can think about right this second is making you feel good, because I don't want you hurting, and because I want to touch you," he said. "Can I? Now is probably not the time and I shouldn't be asking but . . . please."

"What?" She mut have heard him wrong. She twisted her head to look at him. His face appeared sincere. Pleading, even.

"Please. Let me make you feel better. Let me touch this gorgeous body I have in my arms." Warmed by his body, water spread against the side of her neck, touching off explosions of tingles all down her spine.

"N—now? Right here?" What exactly did he have in mind? She couldn't quite imagine but *ohh* every tightening inch of her wanted him. Anything he was thinking of. Her tentacles flexed and released in an urgent rhythm, still wrapped tight around his thighs.

"The divers won't see us. If you're quiet they won't hear us. Won't even know we're here," he said coaxingly.

Oh fuck. A naughty part of her wanted them to hear. Wanted everyone to see whatever he was about to do to her and know they weren't getting it because it was *all for her.* "Yes."

"Yes?" He obviously wanted her clear consent.

She gave it, although she could still hardly comprehend this was actually happening. "Yes. You can touch." *Always yes. It's always been yes. You just never asked.*

Instantly, his hands roamed wildly and he trailed his lips over the curve of her ear, her neck, her bare shoulder. He extended their arms together, meshing their fingers and tracing the sharp tips of her fingernails before wrapping his arms around her again. Her claws didn't seem to bother him at all.

She tilted her lower body to push against his erection. Maybe she'd get to see it this time. Her tentacles hugged him closer. They weren't about to let him get away, greedy things.

"Your body is just . . . killer." His groan vibrated against her back. "I've been wondering about these breasts for years. Three *loong* years," he said, ghosting his hand across her chest.

"Oh. Well good," she said. If he liked breasts, she had *just* the thing for him. They were heavy and hard to find supportive tops for, and when she thought about them at all, it was usually with annoyance. But merely *imagining* his eyes on her bare tits made her burn. She tugged her top down herself, too impatient to wait, letting them pop free.

"Perfect," he said, with reverence. "So damn perfect." He cupped her with his palms, molding her flesh. "Your nipples are the same purple as your lips."

Were they? She'd never bothered thinking about it. But he seemed surprised and delighted at the discovery.

Then he shifted to let his fingertips trail over her skin experimentally, learning her curves. "I always knew you were beautiful. I wish I'd spent more time appreciating it instead of fighting." He stroked and teased as if they had all day to stay right here, touching each other.

She wished he'd spent more time appreciating her, too. Desperately, Marcelline fought and stomped down the little bud of hope that what she'd only dared to dream about was drifting into her reach. It wasn't. This was some . . . strange current carrying them both along after the adrenalin today. A momentary aberration, and then they'd go back to their usual patterns.

For now, she'd kill the hope dead and just enjoy her enemy touching her.

Caspian rubbed lazy, sensual circles around and around her nipples with his thumbs. Against her conscious will, Marcelline bucked in his hold. She couldn't help it. Hot, heavy pleasure flooded her nerve endings. Bliss that he caused, he controlled, playing her with his strong fingers like he owned her during this strange new kind of battle they were engaged in. He moved and she reacted, an instinct for her by now, even though they weren't exchanging blows. Now they traded pleasure, instead.

Her brain shut off entirely, and all thoughts of holding back from him vanished. Without thinking, she let out a moan. "Marcelline."

His fingers tightened on her nipples, pinching hard enough to make her suck in a slug of water her gills struggled to process. "What was that?" he asked.

"Marcelline. My name."

"Oh, you don't know how much I wanted to know that," he panted. "Marcelline. Show me what you need. Show me how you make yourself come."

Her slit. He meant her slit. She wasn't quite like a human woman, and for an instant, she wondered if he would dislike the difference. But she couldn't stop shuddering, and she ached for him to soothe her. With his erection nudging hard against her back, he seemed more than willing to get onboard that plan.

Tentatively she parted her two foremost tentacles, widening them until the spot where a two-legged woman's thighs would come together was exposed. Usually, her slit stayed hidden by her body and enclosed safely. Now, she let it into view, already furled open and throbbing with the need he'd caused.

"Show me." His voice was rough, almost a growl.

She slid her hand along her torso slowly, a bit of bait for him to watch. At her opening, she dipped a finger inside, finding herself already wet and slippery. "Here. Inside, like this."

He kissed the side of her neck and slipped two fingers between her breasts, sliding them down in imitation of her own. Leaving a trail of pure fire in their wake. Gently, he nudged her hand aside. For a long, torturous moment, he traced the lips of her core, tantalizing her with the promise of more. "Here?" he teased.

"Inside, Caspian," she moaned.

"I can't ever resist that damn voice of yours," he said. "Siren."

Without any other warning, he plunged a thick finger inside her, making her hiss with pleasure. Unlike her usual method, he wasn't in a hurry to get her off. No, he rotated and stroked, plunged and retreated, learning her from the inside with excruciating slowness. First one finger, then two.

He palmed her breast with his free hand and tugged her nipple again and oh this was a thousand times better than using her own tentacle and pretending it was him.

Her hips lifted and fell in rhythm with his movements. Her tentacles rocked him against her back, mimicking what she wanted from him, slipping their tips inside his suit wherever they could.

She lifted an arm to wrap it around his neck and arched into him, *demanding* his body as her anchor. Too many sensations at once. She didn't know which way was up anymore. Every single diver could be lined up staring at them, and her pleasure-blinded eyes would tell her nothing. She might even still be moaning, she didn't know.

"Here's something new," he said. She gloried in the rough scrape of his voice, knowing she'd caused it. "What's this, Marcelline? Is this a sweet spot?"

"*Yess,*" she nearly wailed, but the sound caught in her throat. Her tentacles tightened on him, slipping further under the edges of his suit so her suckers could taste his skin, out of her control completely. She threaded her fingers through the hair at the nape of his neck and gripped him tightly. So good. She'd never dared imagine anything like this. He'd found the little bundle of nerves tucked inside her slit. Found it, and curled his fingers, stimulating it.

"Fuck. Fuck. Fuck," she panted.

"It *is* a sweet spot." He groaned into her neck and kept working her, rocking into her back in matching rhythm to his fingers. "So damn hot. So tight and slippery for me."

Her free hand clamped over his wrist, the only solid thing in the world to hold onto as she shattered. She saw nothing, heard nothing, but *felt* everything. The strong tendons shifting under her palm, the heated wall he made at her back, the pure, delirious pleasure dragging her up and up and into a brain-stunning orgasm.

Chapter Seven

Caspian was fairly sure he'd just come inside his super suit. Yeah. The hot spot directly over his groin meant he definitely had. *That* was a first for an encounter with the Sea Bitch.

Except, she wasn't the Sea Bitch now, or ever again. She was *Marcelline*. Marcelline, who had flung herself in front of him and taken the bite meant to maim him. The gorgeous sea creature who embodied pure, fierce strength with her arms held out, her tentacles spread wide to guard him.

He didn't know why the craving to touch her had hit him so hard in that specific moment. His timing hadn't been ideal, underwater, a few kelp fronds away from unsuspecting divers. There might have been a shark circling back around to have another go at eating him. But when he'd wrapped his arms around Marcelline to pull her further into the kelp everything had come to attention and focused on *her*. Terrible timing be damned.

And she was more than he'd ever dreamed. An underwater explosion—hot, wet, slick, *his*.

But now that the high was draining out of him, he could hear the Maritimas Institute divers. If they approached any closer they would see his new obsession; Marcelline's gorgeous bare tits. They'd see his fingers still buried inside her.

A new savage, possessive part of him he'd just discovered didn't want anyone to see her when she was vulnerable and open. He'd blast the divers' eyes out with saltwater streams. Definitely un-heroic behavior, but he didn't care. He'd pleasured her, he'd made her writhe in his arms, *he* was the only one who got to enjoy seeing it.

He lifted her top. "Divers coming. We should move." With regret, he slipped his fingers from her warm, welcoming body. The ocean chilled him like slushy ice after all that scorching heat.

Against his chest, her back stiffened. "Can't stand to be seen with me like this?"

"Not when you're mostly naked, no. That's private. We should get your tentacle looked at, we can—"

"No, *we* can do nothing," she interjected. "I'll take care of my own injuries."

Body and mind united to protest the idea of separating from her. *Loudly*. "No, we really should go to a doctor."

When she slipped out of his arms and turned to face him, her expression was smooth. Unreadable. The way she'd looked at him for three years. It made him inexplicably nervous. "Caspian, there is no *we*. There is nowhere we can go together peacefully and not cause a major news incident."

"If you need medical care, you can go get it. It doesn't matter if I'm with you." She was probably right about the news incident, but he didn't care what reporters said about him anymore. Assholes and anchovies to his image.

She barked a harsh laugh. "No doctor in Ocean City would admit or treat me. They wouldn't know where to start, anyway. And it's not like I can knock on the Maritimas Institute's door and ask about their marine veterinarian. Did one orgasm make you forget? *I am the Sea Bitch*. I am the bad guy. No one helps the bad guy. No one smooches their boo-boos when they get hurt."

"You're not the bad guy anymore, and that isn't true. If they don't know how to help you in Ocean City we could drive to Smallcity and the Supers Hospital." It couldn't be true. She could get the help she needed after a battle. Couldn't she?

Except, he'd never seen or heard of a supervillain in a hospital. Not once.

Her tentacles thrashed, expressing impatience despite her smooth, blank face. "The Smallcity Legion of Heroes would send someone to escort me right out their doors. That's not how our world works," she insisted. "Caspian, you hold all the power here. You are the superhero, the one people love, the one everyone *listens* to. I am what you made me and I always will be."

All of the oxygen had leached out of the ocean somehow. Caspian's gills weren't pulling it in like they should. "Made you? What I . . . made you? How?"

Now her face held an expression, and it was one he wanted to wipe off the earth forever. "Do you remember the first thing you ever said to me?"

He tried to force his sluggish brain back to when he'd been hunting for the villain sinking boats outside Ocean City. Focusing seemed nearly impossible when it felt as if two separate bands had wrapped around his throat, squeezing and squeezing.

After arriving, he'd gotten a distress call from a fishing crew being attacked by something underwater. She'd been there, beneath the waves, and—"You were sinking a boat. I asked something about what you were doing."

Slowly, she shook her head. "*What's a villain like you doing in a deep zone like this?* That's what you asked."

"I thought you were the villain. Was something else out there? Something else was sinking vessels?"

"Nothing was *sinking* those nasty murder vessels, not the way you mean. I was causing slow leaks and making those fuckers drydock for repairs. So the greedy assholes would stop poaching and overfishing. Bet you the Legion forgot to mention that part."

She was right. They hadn't told him that part if they'd even known. But Caspian hadn't searched for any background information himself when he'd arrived in Ocean City. He'd just gone where he was told, all prepared with a witty one-liner. He'd fired it off without thinking what damage a single shot could cause.

"I was so sure I was the hero of my own story," Marcelline said derisively. "The defender of the ocean. Everyone else took one look at me and decided I was the villain. And *you* were the defender against *me*."

The raw pain exposed by her mocking tone slammed into Caspian. Like any other projectile, it opened a gaping hole in him. And *he'd* been the one to launch it. Oh no. Oh, fuck, no. He'd been so wrong . . .

"Did you ever look up the name of that boat, the very first boat you battled with me to save?" she asked.

"No. I didn't," he choked out. He hadn't looked up anything. He'd only assumed.

"Go find it. Go find out about them, what they were ripping off and selling for soup." She shook her head again, making her blue hair float like water weed. "The Legion decided I was your enemy. Everyone else looked at me and agreed. That's all I am now."

"No." If all of that was true, he'd made the biggest mistake of his entire life.

She had never been the villain here.

"*Yes*. That's the only *we* thing about us, Caspian. There are clear lines between 'good' and 'bad'. We've already established which side of the line each of us is standing on. It's too late to change that."

"It's not too late."

She stared at him, clearly wondering what it would take to break through his stubbornness. "You can't . . . erase all of our battles and decide you're okay with me now. Now that you've seen my tits I'm good for more than a fight. Uh-uh. I don't think so. I am your nemesis."

"And you held your own against me all these years," he said, realizing as he spoke how true it was. "You fought back every day and still had time to chase off the greedy fucks I wasn't catching. I wouldn't even be Water Wonder without you. You are so strong, Marcelline. I can't change the mistake I started with, but I can change minds. I can start looking at things more carefully and listen to what you have to say. I can treat you like the hero you are. Let me prove it."

"I can't." Her voice broke and the pieces of it slammed into his heart. "How can I? How can I trust you mean it?"

His own stupidity blocked him from touching her. All he could do was curl his fingers into fists. "Please. You can trust me. Please let me fix this."

"I can't see any way to fix *this*." She gestured wildly, spreading her arms to encompass their world, their powers, and the way heroes and antiheroes worked all at once. "Just leave me alone. Okay? I can't, not right now. I–I have to go take care of this." Her mauled tentacle lifted as a reminder.

His worst fear had always been Sea Bitch getting hurt. Now the nightmare played out before his eyes in vivid color and there was not one powerless hell-deeps thing he could do about it except to watch and take the pain he'd earned.

"Alright," he forced out. "Tell me you'll go to the doctor."

"I can't tell you that. They wouldn't see me."

Then he would be having a conversation with the doctors at Ocean City Health before the end of the day. He dragged in a harsh breath, letting his gills expand to their widest. "At least tell me where I can find you later. Please, tell me where you live."

"Whoa, no. I can't do that, either." Her voice held constrained panic and that made *him* edge closer to the same.

He wanted to use a current to rope her to his side and never let her out of his sight. To drag her through the hospital doors and demand that they heal her *right now*. Hells, he wanted to be able to wrap his arms around her again. "Marcelline. Give me *something*. I'm begging."

"I need to go take care of this tentacle. I'll take care of myself."

Fuck. Fuck, fuck, fuck. He had no way to deny her, not when it was his fault she felt like she couldn't count on anyone else. "Then you know where I'll be. My cave is your cave anytime you want. And my house is two blocks south of the pier, right on the beach. You know where I'm talking about?"

She nodded jerkily, still hugging herself.

"It's the only one with no seawall, and it . . . oh," he paused at the realization. "It's dark blue. The same color as your hair." He was such an idiot. Even his subconscious had known all along how precious she was. He flattened his palms over his eyes and scrubbed, trying to press all his bursting thoughts back inside his skull. "Please. Please at least say you'll come and let me know when you're alright."

"I'll be alright," she said softly, which wasn't an answer at all.

When he removed his hands from his face, she'd already disappeared.

Chapter Eight

Marcelline hovered at the shoreline in front of Caspian's house. Foamy breakers swished gently around her tentacles. Her damaged one still stung, but it was a dull throb compared to the bright flashes of pain from this morning. Already healing.

The rest of her idiotic limbs were trying to sneak across the sand all crafty-like. She trembled with the effort of forcing them to still. A constant swish and murmur from the waves covered the pounding of her hearts. But no one was on this private stretch of beach to hear them, anyway. Thank All the Powers for that.

If it hadn't been so late she wouldn't be here at all. Water Wonder's precious reputation wouldn't survive The Sea Bitch herself waltzing up to his house in broad daylight. There were probably paparazzi camped in the dunes right now, waiting for morning to try snapping pictures of him when he poked his head outside. Gossip papers covered him *incessantly*.

She knew this because she had every article ever written about him bookmarked and saved on her ancient laptop computer, and every single picture the press had managed to capture printed out. A thousand little pieces of him, hoarded together with her memories of their banter. Her collection—*fixation*—was the reason she'd nearly panicked when he asked to come find her lair.

What would the flawless superhero think if he saw the *full size movie poster* prominently featured in her home base? It took up an entire wall of the one dry room left in the evil scientist's—her *"father's"*—ruined underwater facility. Her home.

Marcelline groaned softly and covered her face with the tips of two tentacles.

She'd ruined *everything*. They'd had a routine together. Even though it hadn't included any soft touches or kind words from him, it had been *their* procedure. In their own strange, slightly twisted way, they had belonged only to each other.

She'd never fought any other hero and never wanted to. Every day after their brief battles she'd followed Caspian, desperate just to keep breathing the same water going in and out of his gills. Then she'd been reckless enough, *stupid* enough, to emerge from the shadows and talked to him. As if they could be friends. He'd been her own secret, self-administered, daily dose of poison but what would a concentrated dose of him do? Would his freely given touch kill her in the end—or finally be her antidote?

He'd kissed her. Touched her with reverence. Made her come. And now . . .

Well, now the longing for more felt like it would eat her alive from the inside.

But she couldn't have more. She *knew* she never could. All of the reasons she'd listed to herself over and over still existed. He would always be a superhero. She would always be beneath his status and position as a non-human looking villain.

There would be no happily ever after for them. If they tried strolling off into the sunset together people would assume she was kidnapping him and then the *real* fun would begin when the terrified calls started pouring in to the Legion of Heroes. Marcelline snorted into her suckers, picturing the mass hysteria, then let her tentacles drop.

Standing on the shoreline, knowing every possible door was pre-locked against her, she still couldn't make herself turn around and leave. Instead, she stood frozen, looking longingly at the warm light coming from his windows.

In the dim light of the moon, the blue siding of the house looked even darker. She sucked in a breath, thinking of Caspian's unexpected words—*The same color as your hair.*

Aggravating person. What did that mean? Was that a compliment, somehow? Why would he paint his house any color which reminded him of her?

Sighing, she finally allowed her tentacles to slither forward. She crept to his door and laid the scallop shell she'd brought with her on the wide stone doorstep. The door itself was made of thick, frosted glass. On either side of it, pale blue cloth covered two expansive windows, glowing faintly with the light from inside but still opaque enough to give Caspian privacy. With a little luck, he wouldn't even know she'd been here until tomorrow.

She fussed with the flat shell, moving it to the side a little so he wouldn't step on it and break it when he emerged. Then she straightened, looking over the residence.

This was the closest she'd ever been to it, although she'd watched him walk through this same door from beyond the breaker line an embarrassing amount of times. Standing so near in the secrecy of the dark, she could discover the little touches he'd included in his home. She could absorb the delights of the hidden waves worked into the dark blue stucco, the pots of succulents softening the harsh lines of the walls, the scattering of shells along the windowsills.

Her hand had almost touched the doorbell before she snatched it away.

No. Better to try to return to what they'd had before, what she knew was possible.

She turned and wrenched her wretched tentacles into line, forcing herself back down the shore and into the water.

Behind her, moonlight picked out her hastily scrawled writing on the scallop shell she'd left for him:

I am fine now–M.

###

Caspian completely missed Marcelline's shell message the first time he walked outside in the morning. He walked right past it—twice—on his way to the waterline and back. Only on his second agitated round of pacing did he notice the way the sand above the tideline humped and rippled, as if something had dragged through it. Something with *tentacles*.

He dashed back to his front door and this time the white shell caught his eye. He snatched it, read, and sagged in disappointment. Fine now? Aggravating sea creature. What did *fine* even mean? Marcelline could still be hurting yet say she was *fine*. She could be on her way to the Adriatic sea right now, telling herself a chopped tentacle was only a small nick. She might be anywhere, in any state. Fine meant *nothing*.

She definitely hadn't gone to the hospital. He'd checked. Actually, he'd spent hours last night protesting at the front desk dragon, then complaining to a nurse, then arguing with the shift-lead nurse, then insisting at a doctor, and finally discussing things with the hospital director herself.

All of them had recited variations of the same theme—they had never once seen The Sea Bitch for treatment, and she hadn't been there that evening.

Their averted eyes, cleared throats, and tense posture had also told him they might not have given her care if she *had* slithered through those sliding glass doors. When he'd tried pointing out she wasn't a *monster*, only superpowered just like him, the director had looked honestly confused. The medical motto of *First do no harm* apparently didn't apply to freakishly non-human antiheroes.

Marcelline had tried to tell him.

The scallop shell cracked under Caspian's tightening grip. He forced his fingers to uncurl.

Click click-click.

From either side of his house, the sound of phones and a few old-fashioned digital cameras let him know the press was there, taking pictures. Like always. He didn't need to turn his head to see his regular paparazzi, he knew what they looked like, what they sounded like.

He growled, then spun on his heel and slammed back inside the privacy of his house.

Marcelline was out there, somewhere, injured and alone. Always, always alone. He had droves of fans and photo-hungry journalists following him around. She had nothing. They didn't even see her as human, and it was *his own fucking fault* because he'd treated her like everyone expected him to. They'd slipped into their pre-defined roles and he'd let them do it.

From the very first second he'd seen the splendor in her. She belonged in the ocean, an innate part of it, and he'd always loved the sea. She was power and beauty, unpredictable and calm, violent and merciful, and as alluring as the water she lived in.

And this beautiful, powerful creature clearly didn't feel as if she could come to his house in the daytime, even when he'd explicitly invited her to do so. She'd crept to his door to leave her non-message sometime in the night, probably when he'd still been arguing with the hospital staff.

Why shouldn't she come right to his door? Why *shouldn't* he be able to wrap his arms around her and let the powers-damned cameras have at them?

Because she was the bad guy.

Because they'd spent the last three years fighting.

Because the superhero wasn't supposed to fall in love with the nemesis.

He'd spent the first twenty-two years of his life fitting into his role, accepting his fame, sculpting himself to fit the rules of their world. He'd cared so much what other people thought of him. And all the line-toeing had given him in return was a case of paparazzi as stubborn and itchy as ringworm.

Great. Okay. He was done. For however many years remained to him, he made his own rules. And that meant starting now, his life would include Marcelline. *Openly* include her.

Inside the entryway of his home, Caspian straightened. "Fuck it," he said, surprised at the clear, firm tone in his voice. He tried again. "I don't give a shiver of sharks sexing it up what they think. I don't have even one shit left. They can all fuck right off."

Saying it felt good. It felt like . . . freedom.

Finding his permanent marker took some frantic searching through his office and kitchen drawers, but finally, he'd scrawled his own message on the other side of Marcelline's shell. He propped it carefully in the windowsill, facing out.

Then he went to his bathroom and checked his appearance in the mirror. He looked tired, but his hair lay perfect as always and his eyes were full of fresh excitement. A clean super suit and a splash of cold water took care of his exhaustion.

After a last look in his entryway mirror, Caspian stepped out his front door and waited for the familiar clicking. He stalked towards the closest photographer, then stopped at the edge of his yard and motioned at the man. "Hi. Yes. Hello. You. I need you to come over here."

The man gaped at him from his spot behind a patch of sand lettuce. An old, scuffed silver camera dangled from his fingers, threatening to fall into the dune below any second.

Caspian sighed. "Please come here. I need to talk to your editor."

After checking behind him, then to either side, the man leaned forward hesitantly. "Me? You need my editor?"

"I have a story for them."

Chapter Nine

Six days later, Caspian dragged himself wearily up the beach inside his hidden cavern. As soon as he reached a drier patch of sand, he flopped to the ground and rolled onto his back.

Rex's familiar squeak filled the quiet, and she immediately left her boulder lair. She scrabbled over Caspian to plant herself right in the middle of his chest, her foot claws prickling, antennae waving energetically. She obviously gave him a harsh talking to, but since everything was in lobster, most of the emotional effect got lost.

Probably for the best.

"Sorry. I'm so sorry, Rex." Her crusher claw almost nicked his chin. He couldn't decide if she'd missed on purpose or accidentally.

"I should have come sooner. Sorry, buddy." He'd been trapped in various news conferences, fielding calls, blocking number after number, and answering endless emails. Mostly, he'd been a record on repeat, saying *yes, I was sincere* over and over and over. Every time he'd found a few open hours he'd researched the vessels berthed in Ocean City, their fishing license, catch limits, and how often particular boats had needed repairs over the last four years. Then he'd used every free minute he didn't have searching for Marcelline.

But the villain had been nowhere. Not a sight of her, by him or by any of the—still slightly stunned—residents of Ocean City. This was the longest period he'd gone without seeing her in almost four years and he was *suffering*.

A hero couldn't exist without their villain, Caspian had discovered. Or at least, they didn't want to.

"Sorry. Here. Have a snack." He dug into his pocket and held up the carp he'd caught on the way, but he didn't bother moving as Rex tore into it. *Let her dribble fish bits all over my super suit. No one's here to care.* Marcelline wouldn't see it. Obviously, he'd be lucky if he ever saw her again—

"That's a little gross," an all-too familiar, beautiful voice said. "Not going to lie."

Caspian jackknifed upward so fast Rex went flying off his chest. She clicked at him furiously, then snatched her carp with her grabber claw and dragged it away. He went to pat the lobster apologetically, but completely missed her, because he was staring so hard at *Marcelline*.

Rex fixed him with her eye-stalks, waved her crusher claw slowly, and danced side-to-side. It looked like any other lobster movement to Caspian, but Marcelline's tentacles lashed outward. "Rude!" she snapped.

"Marcelline." Caspian stood, never taking his eyes off of his nemesis.

"Who even taught her that? Did you teach her? Because that is not appropriate for a lobster—"

"*Marcelline.*"

She flashed her gaze to him. "What?"

"I haven't seen you in almost a week and I want to hug you" —*kiss the oxygen out of you*—"but I'm worried you might smack me across the cave if I do."

She narrowed her gorgeous violet eyes at him. "I might do that anyway."

Before he could figure out how to begin talking her out of it she'd slithered across the sand, wrapped her hand behind his neck, and yanked him into a scorching kiss.

The scent of her salty, wave-kissed skin surrounded him. Her lips were hot and open against his, her wet hair stuck to his cheek. She held him tightly to her while her tentacles enfolded everything below his waist in their embrace. *Bliss*.

"How could you?" she panted.

"How could I what," he said, distracted by her limbs as they slithered inside the ankle opening of his super suit to caress him. *What* good ideas they had, the lovely things.

She bent to mouth along the line of his collarbone, then nipped the cord of his neck. The tips of her teeth dug into his skin, barely, just hard enough to make him grunt.

"How could you go to the news like that? That interview wasn't *like* you. Something's wrong with you. It . . . made it sound like you want to work with me, like we'd save the whole ocean together. And we both know that'll never happen—

Caspian wrapped his arms more firmly around her, tugging her against him for another deep kiss. After pulling back, he gazed at her seriously. "We will save the ocean. Together. You and me. From now on."

Marcelline snorted. "You said anyone fishing over the limits, polluting, or poaching should be on notice, that we would retaliate against them. *We*. As in, you and I. You wrote *I Love You, Marcelline* on my shell."

"Yep," he agreed instantly. His desire for this beautiful sea creature flowed in an overwhelming tide which seemed to have no ebb. Only a relentless, endless high tide, surging higher.

"You meant it?" she whispered.

"I mean it. I'll never stop meaning it."

She shivered in his arms. "And you said pre-judging and excluding someone with superpowers based on their looks shows more evil than any supervillain you'd ever heard of."

"Because it does." Desperate, greedy for the feel of her after so many days, he gathered handfuls of her seascape hair, twining the locks around his fingers. "I've been repeating that interview for days, Marcelline. I think everyone is waiting for me to admit I ate a psychedelic sea slug and made up the whole thing. I'd rather talk about your tentacle. How is it? Are you any better?"

Without speaking, she lifted the appendage in question. It still ended as suddenly, but what he remembered as ragged tears had healed to softened edges. It did look much healthier. He sighed in relief and rested his forehead against hers. "Good. That's good."

"Damn it," Marcelline said. "How can I resist you? I can't stay away from you."

"Don't. Don't ever stay away," he begged.

"The Legion won't put up with this. They'll strip your hero status, stop paying your salary–"

"Doesn't matter. And they ought to be taking a real hard look at their methods anyway. Sending out heroes to create villains. That's not what I want to be aligned with." He framed her gorgeous face between his hands, looking deep into her eyes. She needed to hear what he had to say, and she needed to believe him, because he wasn't going anywhere without her after this. "I'm on *your* side now, Marcelline. Whatever team you're on, it's mine too."

Her lips parted in surprise, showing her razor-sharp teeth. Predator fangs. She didn't resemble ordinary people because she'd been perfectly formed to live in and guard their beloved ocean. If no one else could see it, he'd force them to.

Smiling, he brushed a kiss against the corner of her mouth. "I'm with you," he repeated, trailing his lips up her cheek, kissing the curve of it, and then her brow. "From now on."

Her breath puffed unsteadily against his cheek while her hands clenched and unclenched at his waist, bunching up the stretchy material of his suit. "On my side," she said, roughly. "I've never . . . I don't know what that's like."

"You do now."

The suckers on her tentacles left soft, *oh-so-torturous* touches against his bare calves. It was like being surrounded by tiny mouths giving miniscule kisses *all over him*. He'd never imagined anything so erotic in his life.

"What do you say?" he asked. "Want to protect the ocean together?"

Hopefully, she couldn't feel the pounding of his heart against her chest. She'd know how nervous he was, waiting for her to raise her face and deliver his fate.

Chapter Ten

Marcelline could hardly believe the words coming from Caspian's mouth. If there hadn't been plenty of phosphorescence in the cave to light his face, she might have convinced herself her ears were sending delusions right to her brain.

But no, his lips shaped the sounds giving her . . . everything. All she'd ever dreamed of.

She'd imagined one day *possibly* being Water Wonder's dirty little secret. The pinnacle of her hopes had been a good tension relieving hate-fuck after their battles. In the dark, probably underwater, never to be spoken of.

Instead, she'd read his interview in the little local paper, **Ocean Point of View**. Then she'd printed it out and read it again, twice, while the paper shook in her hands. Plainly, openly, explicitly, Water Wonder had claimed The Sea Bitch as an ally.

He'd made her sound like some kind of unsung champion, fighting all alone against the forces of greedy overfishing *and* the uncaring Legion at the same time. He'd bluntly *threatened* anyone who wanted to stand in her way or treat her badly. A hero, threatening people. What had their world come to?

Every major news outlet had picked up the breaking story and she'd waited, day by day, for Caspian to take it all back. She'd scoured the internet for his retraction and apology, while he kept stunning her by committing even *harder*.

How can I? How can I trust you mean it? She'd asked him that day in the kelp.

How about manifestly shattering his image for her? How about breaking ties with The Legion of Superheroes so firmly he'd almost dared them to exile him? How about insisting to all of Ocean City that their villain was actually a hero?

She lifted her face to find Caspian watching her closely. He didn't twitch, didn't seem to even breathe as he waited for her answer. He held the sides of her face, refusing to let her go.

Trust didn't come easily to her and she had trouble believing this incredible change in Caspian's heart would last . . . but she could be brave enough to reach out and take what he was offering. She could at least try. "Yes. I say yes."

An enormous grin spread across his beloved, familiar face. "We're working together now? We're not fighting?"

"Yes," she forced out the word around the squeezing in her chest. "Not fighting."

"No more nemesis?"

"No more." As always, when she was near Water Wonder her ribs felt like they were cracking inward, compressing her chest until she thought her hearts might surrender. This time, she let them. Everything she'd wished from him had somehow become hers. So it was only right for Marcelline to admit she had always been his.

She licked her lips. "I only . . . only ever wanted to be yours. Nemesis or anything else. It didn't matter. I didn't fight you because I hated you. I only battled because it was ours. Our thing. And it was all we had."

Oh, she was mucking this up. But her hearts had dragged behind him for so long, and if he realized it, he could puncture them both with one sharp word.

He spread his thumbs beneath her jaw, gently raising her mouth for another kiss. "We can try having more than fighting, instead. We can have *everything*."

"More kisses?" she asked hopefully.

"Definitely."

Tenderly, his fingers swept down her neck, her shoulders, her arms, making her tremble. "And more touching?" she asked. Might as well ask for the moon and tides while fate seemed to be in a giving mood.

"All the touching. Maybe, if, if you're ready, we could try sex? I've never, um, before." He stuttered adorably, but his hands stayed steady as he worked towards her breasts. "Somehow, two legs just never did it for me. My kink is definitely tentacles."

She smiled. Her tentacles, for once in accord with her brain, pulled Caspian even closer, trying to nudge aside more of his stretchy suit. "I never have before, either," she said. "We can figure it out together."

"Together," Caspian repeated. "I like the sound of it."

And in his hidden cavern under the sea, Water Wonder kissed The Sea Bitch in a way that said this villain would forever after have her happy ending.

Sneak Preview: The Sidekick and The Supervillain, by SE White

Chapter One

Michaela's secret identity turned out not to be such a well-kept secret. Bad enough, she'd been identified at the urgent care where she worked. Worse, she now had to figure out how to swear him to confidentiality or she'd lose her job. Worst of all, *The Evil Bane* was the one to figure it out.

A supervillain who'd come up with a hyperbole like *that* had no business being smart enough to figure out her alter-identity.

"You're the sidekick," he said again. "The one with a name you need a thesaurus for." He snapped his fingers, gazing at the ceiling. As if the words he needed would be imprinted up there on an encouraging cat poster for patients. *Hang in there, sick friend. My alter-ego is the Amiable Accomplice! You're in good hands.*

"You're always with Furia. I'd swear you're her sidekick. Wait, I'll remember in a minute," he insisted. "I think that shot you gave me is kicking in and making me forgetful. My arm feels better, though."

You're always with Furia...

Michaela breathed through the throbbing pain of that thought and ignored the supervillain. If he thought he'd get another chance to see her fighting beside The Fabulous Furia he had another think coming. Her days of trailing along as the world's most useless sidekick were over.

She bustled around, avoiding his eyes while she laid out sterile gauze packs, sealed saline bottles, the glove boxes, and large gauze pads in case they had to debride his wound. Rather than speak to him, she brought up all of his charts on the computer system.

The Evil Bane didn't require another person to keep a conversation going, though. He rambled out loud, trying different alliterations, and musing different alliterative rhymes.

She tuned him out. He was no more interesting than the training dummy she'd practiced on to get her Licensed Practical Nurse certificate. Okay, flabby rubber dummies didn't have those rock hard abs. Or those luscious, tuggable sable locks. Seriously, what brand of conditioner did he use? But the principle stood. He was no more than a practice dummy to her right now.

"Let's check your blood pressure," Michaela said cheerfully. She slipped the cuff over his uninjured arm, avoiding those deep, dark eyes at the same time. He obviously thought she'd help him shatter her cover voluntarily, maybe if he smoldered enough.

"The Cordial Caretaker. . ." he tried. "No, the Affectionate Amigo? *Oww.*"

She could just see his glare out of the corner of her eye. Delicately, she adjusted her fingers so she wouldn't touch any part of his skin while she held the diaphragm down to listen to his artery close and open. The nitrile gloves she was never without slid greasily along her fingertips with every tiny adjustment.

For one scary second she had to fight down an unfamiliar urge to rip the damn suffocating gloves off and just *touch* the world around her like any other being.

"Does it really need to be that tight? I mean, really?"

Michaela angled her head away so he couldn't see her face. Rolling eyes was forbidden bedside behavior—even when you were treating The Evil Bane. She released the pressure, listened and counted, and finally took the dreaded air-pressured torture device off of his arm.

Then she left all common sense, training, and reality behind and stripped off her sweaty, constricting gloves. *With a patient close enough to touch.*

Tossing them in the trashcan gave her a slightly terrifying thrill of triumph.

Chapter Two

If she thought about the sin she was committing she'd freak out, so instead Michaela focused on entering patient stats.

"One-twenty over eighty," she muttered, finding the right entry in the laptop sitting open on the counter.

You took your gloves off what are you doing *your gloves are off!*

"One-twenty...over..." there was the correct spot. She tapped it in before the numbers left her head, fighting the urge to flex her shamefully bare fingers. Then she leaned closer to peek at the pulse oximeter capping his slender forefinger. O2 Sat hovered at ninety-six so no worries there, but his pulse fluctuated wildly. "And one-oh-five. Hmmm."

"What?" The Evil Bane narrowed his eyes at her. "What *hmmm*?"

She finished entering his heart rate without answering. Anxiety built and built until her brain screamed with it.

Gloves you have to be wearing gloves you can't touch him put your gloves back on!

"You said two different numbers back to back. Is that normal? Am I normal? What does that mean, Kindly Comrade?"

Somehow Michaela forced herself to stop chanting *gloves you can't ever take off your gloves!* internally and focus on her patient. "There's nothing to be worried about," she told him. "One-twenty over eighty was your blood pressure. That's completely average."

He appeared faintly insulted.

"And your heart rate is" —she watched the monitor jump from one hundred and five to one hundred, then back to one hundred and one— "a hundred and five beats per minute. That's a bit faster than normal, but you *are* in urgent care. People often have an elevated heart rate under stress. It's all common. Don't worry." She dug a new pair of gloves out of her front pocket and tugged them on in defeat.

He tried a grin. It wasn't his usual, cutting, evil-genius grin. Not the one she remembered seeing as he traded banter with Furia. "Okay, Benevolent Buddy. If you say so."

She barely restrained a snort. "Sir, I think you have me confused with someone else." *Benevolent Buddy.* "Let's take another look at your arm," she suggested.

"Oh, no. No, thanks. Let's not look."

Tilting her head sideways, she said, "If you won't let me look at it, the doctor is still going to anyway."

"Could she not? Or he not? Whoever. Just not. Could we just numb me up really good and send me home?" He flashed the hopeful half-grin again. But he kept his gaze carefully away from the scorched, weeping furrow high on his left bicep.

"With possible contaminants in the wound? So you can get infected and have to come back?" she gave him a gentle, yet impatient look. The same look Fabulous Furia gave Michaela whenever she asked to come back her up in a battle. "If this wound gets infected, you'd have to come back and the doctor would have to *cut it back open* to let all the pus drain."

He winced and shifted on the narrow hospital cot.

"After we cut it back open we'd have to irrigate it," she went on, merciless as winter wind. "That means flushing it over and over to get the infected material out. *Then* we'd have to *scrape* away the dead tissue, which is called debriding, with a tiny toothbrush-looking thing and try to dig out any pockets of—"

"Ooo-kay!" He waved his good arm in emphatic *stop* circles. "We don't need any more details." He twisted his mouth into a sour curve. "You can look at it."

Grinning, she stepped around the cot to his side and leaned forward. She'd kept insisting. And she'd *won*. It was a first for her.

"But don't touch it!" He jerked his neck and head away.

"I won't touch it," she said. He might be one of the most skittish patients she'd ever seen in here. When he relaxed a little she couldn't resist adding, "The doctor will."

As she examined the burn she leaned closer, but she was careful not to touch. Even with nitrile gloves on she had to be cautious. And anyway he'd asked her not to. "What were you doing? How did a burn give you such...slashed edges?"

Burns typically had a rounded shape, originating from the contact spot and spreading out. This looked like he'd somehow sliced himself with an incredibly hot knife, cauterizing as it cut. Overall the laceration was fairly small, maybe eight or nine centimeters long, but it looked nasty.

He muttered something in response. Sounded like *spearmint*.

She tilted her head up to ask what he meant and she was only a breath, the barest touch away from that gorgeous face. He looked so kissable at this distance. She had to tamp down a surprising urge to nip his full lower lip before she kissed her way up to those sharply defined cheekbones—*No, Michaela. Bad, Michaela.*

He'd been leaning over to watch her as she examined his wound—*not* thinking about kisses. She lurched back a step and tilted her head away.

This time he gave her a *real* Bane grin. Cocky, overconfident, sexy as all hells. She'd never known the color of his eyes or how amazing his bone structure was, not through the obnoxious Evil Bane mask he wore. But the mask only covered the top half of his face. She'd always thought it was to show off that handsome square jaw, because yeah, he knew he was handsome. And oh, she knew that seductive grin.

Without her approval, her traitorous insides fluttered and her mouth turned up into an answering smile.

"I've got it," he said abruptly, his eyes lighting up. "I remember. You're the Amiable Acccom—"

She straightened her hand flat in front of his nose. "I am not *the* accomplice, or *an* accomplice, or an amigo, or a buddy. I really think you have me confused with someone else. I need to ask you to stop, sir. You'll get me in trouble." Darting over, she peered out the small window in the examining room door.

Dr. Imark was approaching down the tiled hallway. She had seconds.

She dashed back, leaned closer, and lowered her voice. "Everyone knows you can't trust Empowered to work in a hospital. They might accidentally hurt someone or attract a villain. *Everyone* knows that. Please, Bane. Let's just focus on your injury."

Their eyes locked. He looked unconvinced and she *could not* have that.

Normal Michaela instinct hunched her shoulders, muscles twitching in preparation for turning away. She refused. This job was important to her. Everything in her needed to stay, to help people, and for that she *had* to keep her status as Empowered a secret.

"Please, Bane. Just forget it." Her heart boomed in her ears once, twice, three times. Everything shrank to the two of them, bolted together, waiting to see who would break first.

Finally, he gave her one tiny nod.

"What do we have here, Michaela?" Dr. Imark's big, booming voice entered the room even before she did.

Sound and color flooded back in, like someone had hit the button to un-mute the room around them. She blinked and tried to focus, grateful the pulse oximeter wasn't on *her* finger.

"Ahhh...oh, it looks like...a deep partial-thickness burn. Combined with some laceration." She lifted her gloved hand to point. "Some edema at what looks like the edge of the burn here. Blistering here and here. Patient's blood pressure is normal. Heart rate a little elevated. I already gave him a topical shot to numb the area but we might want to give him one more."

"And who are we treating today?" Dr. Imark gave The Evil Bane a friendly smile as she moved to the sink to wash her hands.

"Ivan," he told her. "Ivan O'Reilly."

Michaela couldn't stop the snort and had to clap a hand over her mouth. She had skimmed right over that part of his chart. His abs had been a tad distracting. But of course he wouldn't check into the facility all barefaced under his evil name.

Ivan O'Reilly. Her side twinged from holding in the laugh that wanted to burst out. He looked like the furthest thing from an *Ivan* or an *O'Reilly* and of course that's why he'd chosen it as his alter-ego.

Both of them stared at her, Doctor Imark with amazement and Bane with one side of his mouth tucked up. His cheek dimpled, which she considered deeply unfair to females and fems everywhere and herself in particular.

"All right then, Ivan, let's get you fixed up," Dr. Imark said, giving Michaela a *do-you-need-to-go-on-break-now* look.

Behind Dr. Imark The Evil Bane winked and Michaela gave him an unimpressed look, even though she could feel the heat of a blush brushing her face.

Chapter Three

Hiro gritted his teeth and tried harder to ignore the pounding ache. The shot had helped. Some kind of topical anesthetic goop around the edges of his burn eased the pain even more. Dr. Imark had been as gentle as she could. But the ghost of agony still haunted his entire arm, crawling through his bicep, creeping up his spine to make him twitch.

Pain had never been something he handled well. He loathed shots. Hated hospitals. Avoided the dentist like a teeny bop concert with glitter cannons. Even though he hadn't watched The Amiable Accomplice and Dr. Imark work his imagination was highly active and his stomach squirmed at the mental images of what they'd been doing as they cleaned his arm.

Especially after that lecture about scraping off dead tissue. Ugh. She knew damn well how gross it sounded and she'd used it against him without a qualm.

She was so pretty, and so underhanded. His very favorite combination.

Definitely, he couldn't trust his nurse. She'd done something to him. It had to have been her. Hiro flexed his fingers. For a second–no, the breath of a second–his hands had felt wrong. Out of nowhere, he'd had this terrible *urge* to put gloves on, to cover up his skin. *Gloves?*

Even stranger, he knew the feeling had nothing to do with him or what he'd been thinking at the time. It had been foreign, separate, intrusive. And he had a strong suspicion it had to do with the sidekick treating him.

What exactly were The Amiable Accomplice's powers again? No one had ever said or specifically listed them out on one of those obnoxious talk show segments, and it only now occurred to him to wonder why...

He caught her checking out his bare chest again and smirked, stealing another look at her nametag. *Michaela.* The Amiable Accomplice was named Michaela. Immediately, she shifted her eyes to scowl at the bandage she was holding and lifted her chin up, pretending he hadn't caught her doing anything. The queasiness rocking his stomach settled a little.

Who would have guessed the Amiable Accomplice worked at an Urgent Care? And why was he even surprised? Superheroes had a *saving-people* thing. Of course they'd do it on their downtime, too. No matter how frowned upon it was.

He thought of her wide eyes and pleading expression when he'd figured it out. She really hadn't wanted him to know.

Please, Bane.

He wanted to hear those words again. Exactly those words, but with a different inflection. A naked inflection. A *please, Bane give me more* kind of nuance. When that gorgeous black hair was spread out all over his pillows and he was in the middle of exploring every centimeter of her smooth skin. And those big eyes were wide with pleasure, instead of worry.

She'd called him *Bane*. She knew who he was—his villain identity, anyway. He'd only come up against Fabulous Furia and her sidekick twice over the last five years. The Amiable Accomplice had mostly been kept in the background, watching him trade blows with her superhero while she kept his bots busy. But she still recognized him.

Hiro was never going to complain when a pretty girl remembered his villain identity. Even if she worked alongside one of the most self-righteous superheroes in the city.

"—how it happened?"

"Hmm?" Hiro tore his eyes away from his nurse. Again. "I'm sorry, what?"

The Doctor gave him a dry smile. "I said, did you have any luck remembering how it happened? It's an unusual burn."

I'm for damn *sure not admitting in front of Michaela that I was testing laser-eye-proof glass and didn't check the angles before I fired and the laser ricocheted back on* my own arm.

He gave the Doctor his best sunny, sincere, open look. "I guess I just wasn't paying attention when I made my toast this morning."

"Toast," she repeated.

"The toaster gets really hot. Those edges are killer. I knocked into it and it was going to fall off the counter and I think I panicked a little. Tried to nudge it back with my arm. Clumsy."

"The toaster did it," she said. The absolute flatness of the Doctor's voice made it clear, she was not amused. "So it wasn't, for instance, a deadly new type of weapon your employer might, as a random example, have you testing out?"

The fight not to let the insult show on his face was strong, but all internal. Alright, so he didn't actually have any minions and had to do all his own testing. Still. Assumptions hurt.

In the far corner of the room, where she was carefully disposing of the bloody pads and towels, Michaela's shoulders shook. When she glanced his way her eyes sparkled with the laughter she struggled to keep bottled.

"I would *never* work for one of those terrible, evil villains," he said primly. True, in the most literal sense. Minions would be working for *him*, someday. "It was the toaster."

"Sure. Okay. Dastardly little things." Dr. Imark shook her head. "We'll have to watch out for more toaster injuries. Well, you're all set to go, Ivan. You've got your discharge papers?" the Doctor asked.

He tapped the sheaf of papers he'd dropped at his side and nodded.

"And you know what you should be concerned about?"

"Any increasing pain, any seepage through the bandages, swelling, and any dizziness, fever, vomiting, or nausea." He reeled it off and made a face. Vomiting was possibly his least favorite thing in the whole world, and that included all the superheroes in Smallcity.

"Alright then. See the receptionist to check out on your way to the door. And come right back if you feel concerned about anything. Don't forget to pick up those antibiotics." She was already on her way to the door, tapping away at her tablet, most likely checking details for the next patient.

"Thanks, Dr. Imark," he said.

She waved a hand briefly and disappeared.

Hiro didn't know how they did it, these good people. Working to someone else's schedule eight to ten hours a day, whiny patients demanding things for every one of those hours, bodily fluids everywhere, barely enough pay to justify any of it. *No, thank you.*

He flicked away those thoughts and smiled over at the resident sidekick. He'd never guessed before today that one of his kinks would be Sexy Nurse, but he was definitely into those ankle length scrubs. "So, your name is Michaela."

She crossed her arms and gave him a flat stare.

"It's on your name tag," Hiro pointed out helpfully.

"Unfortunately, it's a policy," she said, glancing at the tag. "I thought about getting something less obvious like, *The Amiable Accomplice, TOTALLY not in disguise as your nurse, have a nice day.*"

Real appreciation flavored his laugh. "When do you get off work, Michaela?"

The smile in her eyes snuffed out. "No."

"I didn't even ask yet."

"Still no. Supervillains and sidekicks don't mix."

"They could." He raised his eyebrows.

"But they don't. Opposite sides, opposite goals. You hurt people for a living, Bane."

Her voice wobbled and her shoulders curved inward protectively. But she kept her chin up, looking him right in the eyes. The contrast, on top of all her other mysteries, only interested him more.

"Only a little." Even as the words left his mouth he knew it was the wrong thing to say. Too nonchalant. "I'm more in the line of providing...things to people who need them. Not hurting people."

"The things you provide kill people."

Irritation wiped away any traces of his smile. "I have *never* killed anyone. Or provided anything that does."

She lifted both brows in a look which clearly stated, *bold claim*, and shook her head. "Bane, you're charming, and funny, and really good looking. But this is not happening."

Edging his way off of the crackly thin paper of the table, Hiro sent her an ironic look. She couldn't have realized—being told he couldn't do something always fired him up to do exactly that thing.

Challenge accepted.

"I'll be seeing you," he warned. And with one last considering look over his shoulder, he left.

About the Author

SE White is an independent author of contemporary SciFi and historical romance. From characters stumbling into love in the wild west of 1870s Nevada, to supervillains falling hard for heroes, to characters running as fast as they can away from their Soulmates in an alternate modern universe, there's something fun for every reader. SE loves writing the quirky, the sarcastic, the fluffy, and all the niche romance tropes leading to a happily ever after. Guaranteed. She lives and writes in Nevada, USA where she enjoys watching probably unhealthy amounts of Great British Bake Off and spending entirely too much time rating alien romance books on #bookstagram.

Read more at https://www.sewhitebooks.com.